How to Draw
WIZARDS, DRAGONS AND OTHER MAGICAL CREATURES

Barbara Soloff Levy

DOVER PUBLICATIONS, INC.
Mineola, New York

International Standard Book Number

ISBN-13: 978-0-486-49928-4
ISBN-10: 0-486-49928-6

Manufactured in the United States by Courier Corporation
49928601
www.doverpublications.com

Note

Learning to draw wizards, dragons, and other magical creatures is easier than it seems. Follow the simple steps in this book, and you will also discover how to draw a charming princess and a knight in armor, as well as a scary goblin, a friendly leprechaun, and a genie in a bottle!

Each page has four steps (except for the last page of the book, which has a spider and its web). The second, third, and fourth steps add details to the first step. The last step shows you the completed drawing.

It's a good idea to start sketching using a pencil with an eraser, in case you change your mind about part of your picture. You can trace each step first to get a feel for drawing. Then try it on your own. Use the Practice Pages opposite each of the drawing pages, too. *Pay attention to the dotted lines—they should be erased when you have done the last step of the drawing.*

When you are pleased with your drawing, you can go over the lines with a felt-tip pen or colored pencil. If you are not pleased with the drawing, keep working at it, erasing and then drawing in new lines. After you complete your drawings, you can enjoy them even more by coloring them in.

Of course, you can create new drawings using the skills you have learned in this book. Feel free to use your imagination to create magical creatures of your own!

Practice Page

8 Dragon

Practice Page

Practice Page

14   Dragon

Practice Page

Practice Page

Practice Page

Practice Page

Practice Page

Practice Page

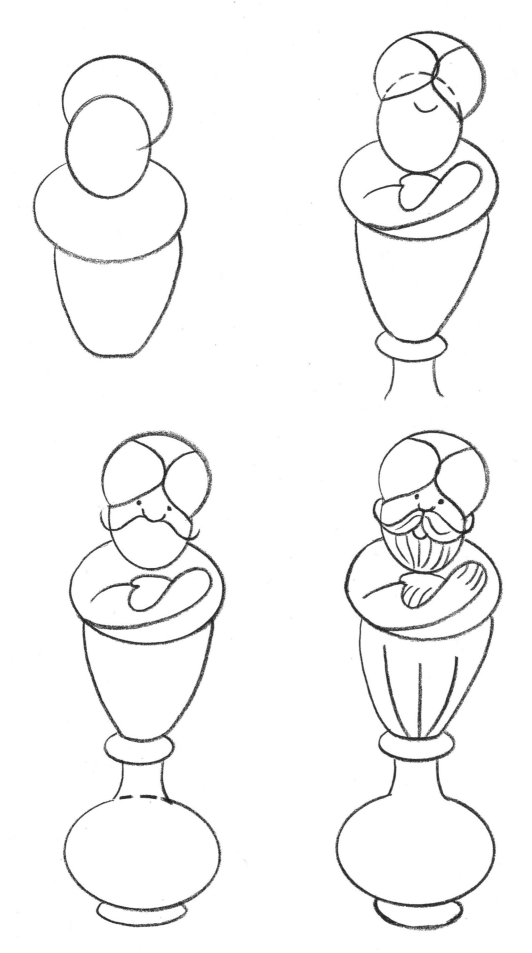

Practice Page

Practice Page

28   Fairy

Practice Page

Practice Page

32   Goblin

Practice Page

38 Troll

Practice Page

Practice Page

Practice Page

46 Leprechaun

Practice Page

50 Unicorn

Practice Page

Practice Page

54 Bat

Practice Page

Practice Page